THIS BOOK BELONGS TO:

Who's learning all the colors of the rainbow!

For Ben & Miranda
who as little ones both found
learning their colors tricky!
Love you both to bits M xxx

One Grey Day

Published by Crane Books in 2021

Crane Books Ltd
The Red House, 10 Market Square
Amersham, Buckinghamshire, HP7 0DQ, UK

Text and illustrations © Daryl Stevenson 2020

A CIP Catalogue Record of this title is available from the British Library

isbn: 978-1-911060-43-7

Printed in China

ONE GREY DAY

WRITTEN AND ILLUSTRATED BY DARYL

One grey day Stanle
and Grace were ou
strolling in th
drizzly rai
when …

"Grace, look! What's that?"

"Oooooh, I don't know ...
Let's go and find out"

"NO, GRACE. Let's NOT
do that!" said Stanley as
he hopped quickly off
her back.

"Well you wait here
Stanley, and I'll go
and investigate!"

Stanley looked on anxiously as Grace disappeared into the . . .

Well Grace had never seen anything like it ...
It was soooooooooooooooooo beautiful!

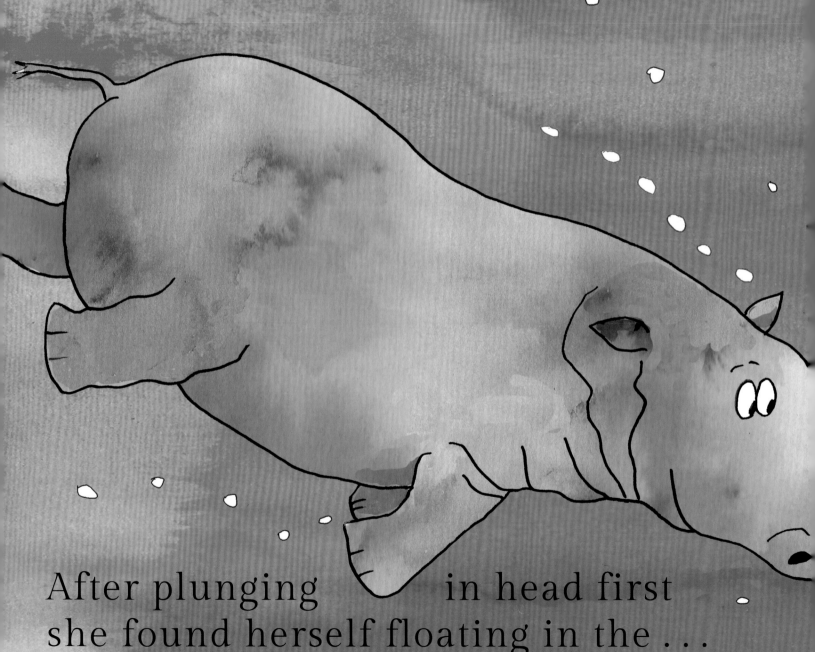

After plunging   in head first
she found herself floating in the ...

PURPLE

She paddled on cheerfully through the ...

PINK

After a beautiful somersault,
Grace did backstroke through the ...

She blew BIG bubbles into the ...

ORANGE

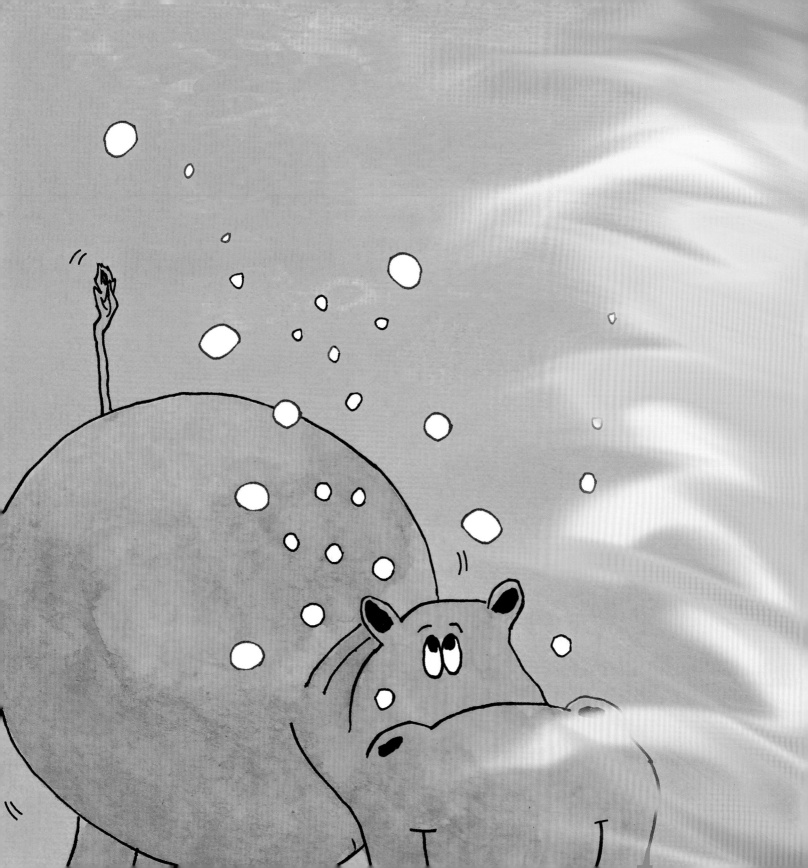

Then she BURST into the ...

YELLOW

...floated gracefully
through the...

GREEN

…UTIFUL

I'm on my way, Grace!"

Stanley took a deep
breath and flew into
the rainbow after
his friend …

"Oh Grace, you ARE beautiful . . . and so am I!

AND . . .

look at my
jolly umbrella!"

The rain
had
stopped and
the sun had
come out.

So Grace
and Stanley,
holding his beautiful
umbrella, strolled on!

Help Stanley work out what colors his friends are . . .